Holiday Short Stories

Morbier Impossible
A Second Chance
The Magic of Sharing
The Case of the Disappearing Gingerbread City
The Lucia Crown
Down the Memory Aisle

The Magic of Sharing

by R.W. Wallace

Copyright © 2020 by R.W. Wallace

First published in WMG Publishing's 2020 *Holiday Spectacular*

Cover by R.W. Wallace

Cover Illustration 198159104 © Lilkar | Dreamstime.com

Cover Illustration 191647094 © Jeannadraw | Dreamstime.com

All characters and events in this book, other than those clearly in the public domain, are fictitious and any resemblance to real persons, living or dead, is purely coincidental.

All rights reserved. No part of this publication may be reproduced, distributed, or transmitted in any form or by any means, including photocopying, recording, or other electronic or mechanical methods, without the prior written permission of the publisher, except in the case of brief quotations embodied in critical reviews and certain other noncommercial uses permitted by copyright law.

www.rwwallace.com

ISBN ebook: [978-2-493670-00-7]

ISBN paperback: [979-10-95707-99-8]

AUTHOR OF *MORBIER IMPOSSIBLE*

R.W. WALLACE

the MAGIC of SHARING

A HOLIDAY SHORT STORY

The Magic of Sharing

Three cold noses pressed up against the windowpane, we watch as the family finishes off their Christmas dinner. There's nothing but bones left of the smoked and salted lamb —the *pinnekjøtt*—someone left half a potato in the dish and both the father and mother have been eying it but seem to decide they really are too full, and the three-year-old seems to think Christmas has come an hour early because he's allowed to finish off the dish of mashed rutabaga with his fingers.

The parents have finished two bottles of Christmas beer each—the kind with *nisser* on them, making the fact that we're out here starving just a little bit worse—while the kids are drinking *julebrus*, the red soda that's only available this time of year.

Toward the back of the room, the fireplace is quietly crackling in one corner and the Christmas tree calmly waiting its turn in the other.

They went all out with the tree this year. They always pick one out from their own forest, but since the ultimate goal of that forest is for the trees to grow tall and straight to be cut down and sold, they usually take one of the feeble ones, one that won't bring in a profit later. This usually means that their Christmas tree is halfway dead, twisted, or maimed in some way.

The tree currently in the corner almost reaches the ceiling, is straight as an arrow, and has branches on all sides. The look the mother gave the father when he brought it in made me think this was his early present for his wife—their tree was going to be a beauty this year.

The entire family spent yesterday morning decorating it. The father put in the lights and the star on the top. The mother did the Norwegian flags, the tinsel, and the breakable decorations.

The three kids did all the rest: woven baskets, angels, nisser, baubles, and some unidentifiable ones that they'd made themselves.

All the while, we were standing out here in the cold, looking in.

Nissemor, my wife, can't seem to stop staring at the tree. She's always had a weak spot for the lights, loving how they give the entire room a soft glow at night when everyone has gone to bed. They remind her of the open starry sky, which she can spend hours gazing at when the weather allows. Here, they're in a setting that screams of the love this family has for each other and the holiday. Anything representing love has Nissemor's heart.

Tulla, my daughter, has her eyes on the presents. Not because she wants to open them—we nisser have never had any use for the toys, clothes, or books inside those packets—but because she's anticipating the moment the children will open them. Tulla loves playing, loves a good prank, loves anything that will make a child scream in joy. And those colorfully packaged gifts always deliver.

"Is it time for the presents now, Dad?" Her face is squished into the window to the point where her nose is completely flat and even her lips and forehead are pressed to the glass.

"They've finished eating, so it's time for the presents, right?" She places her palms on the glass and closes her eyes. "Please, please, please," she whispers fervently. I put a hand on her shoulder, giving it a little squeeze. "They'll get to the presents, Tulla." I swallow a gulp. "They haven't had dessert yet."

Her knitted red hat and matching sweater are covered in snow from when she made a snow angel on the roof earlier. Her gray felt pants are probably wet but so long as she doesn't complain, I won't say a thing.

Nissemor tears her gaze away from the tree and we share a look. This is always the most painful part of the night for us.

This used to be *our* moment.

We nisser don't really need human food to sustain ourselves. Well, no, we do. But we don't need the humans to *give* it to us, we just help ourselves. We're no bigger than your regular house cat and don't need much to get by, so the humans never notice if one potato goes missing here and one piece of cheese is suddenly a little smaller there.

What we do need is their belief in us.

And that has been waning dangerously over the last few years.

On the farm next door, the Jensen family, there used to be a nisse family much like ours. They lived in the hayloft and helped out mostly with the cattle. Their young son, especially, had a way with the calves that had saved more than one life. Then, five years ago, the humans had their own son, a squealing and loud thing they named Ole.

The year Ole turned two, they decorated the entire barn with Christmas lights, adding more as they saw how much the little boy loved them. When he turned three, they added a Santa Claus with a sleigh. The kid *adored* the reindeer.

Last year, they got a neighbor to dress up as Santa and bring gifts.

We haven't seen the nisse family since.

We don't need much but we need their belief. And the ultimate show of faith comes on Christmas Eve.

In the good old days, everybody knew the drill. Be nice to the nisse on Christmas Eve and give him his porridge, and he'll help you out around the farm the entire year. Don't give him his food, and he'll do the opposite. He'll mess with the animals, move your hay over to your neighbor's barn, make sure the crops don't grow.

I haven't pulled any mean tricks like that since I was a kid. Haven't dared to.

Despite not having had porridge in over twenty years.

But they still remember us. They at least *sort of* believe. Which is why we're still here.

Inside the house, the mother is preparing the dessert in the kitchen while the father takes a seat on the couch, the children settling in around him.

"Oh, they're going to read the story!" Tulla does a quick pirouette before squeezing her nose back to the window.

Indeed, they're reading the story. The one about the nisse and the fox, where the nisse convinces the fox not to steal any of the humans' chickens on Christmas Eve. Where he shares his porridge with the animal instead.

It's a sweet story—and probably why we're still here. The question is how long it'll last.

I put my arms around Nissemor as we watch the father turn the pages and the children's reactions. The six-year-old daughter, especially, seems completely caught up in the story and frequently stops her father to ask questions.

When the story is done, the dessert is on the table. Like every year, it's rice pudding, made from porridge and whipped cream.

The father gives the mother a kiss before sitting down. The oldest starts sprinkling his dessert with sugar. The youngest puts his hand directly into his plate, earning him a half-hearted rebuke from both parents.

The six-year-old doesn't take her seat. She stands next to her chair, staring at the plate.

"Why aren't they eating?" Tulla whispers. "They have to eat, so they can finish eating, so they can get to the presents. That big one in the back is a sled, I'm sure of it!"

The girl doesn't move, even when her mother clearly tells her to take her seat so they can all have their dessert.

A discussion ensues, apparently having something to do with the rice pudding. I wish I could hear what they're saying, but the only way to hear them is by going through the attic, and that would mean missing out on too much.

The mother's frustration seems to grow as the daughter refuses to comply, but I notice the father's features softening. When his wife is clearly about to lose her temper, he shoots one quick glance at the couch—where the storybook was discarded—and gets up from his seat.

He takes his daughter into the kitchen. They get a plate. Fill it with porridge. They heat it in the microwave. Sprinkle with sugar and cinnamon. And the daughter puts the biggest dollop of butter I have ever seen in the very center.

"Is that...?" Nissemor has a hand over her mouth and her breath hitches.

I'm afraid to get my hopes up.

"What are they *doing*?" Tulla says. "Why do they need porridge on top of the rice pudding? Can't they just eat? Get to the gifts already?"

Tulla was born the year of our last portion of porridge. She has never tasted it, not the real thing, the one given to us by humans. She doesn't understand the significance, as she's never felt the magic of real belief. She has spent her entire life in this half-life existence we've had for the last twenty years.

Could it really be...?

Nissemor and I both hold our breaths as the father tells his daughter to put on her winter jacket and snowshoes, then gently places the bowl of porridge in her hands before opening the front door for her.

"She's going to do it," Nissemor whispers in awe.

The father closes the door behind his daughter and walks over to our window to keep an eye on her. We jump down from our spot to hide next to a pile of firewood. The humans usually can't see us anyway but it's best to always play it safe.

"What's going on?" Tulla whispers.

"You'll see," I tell her. "Just keep quiet, darling, and you'll see."

The girl very carefully walks to the barn, the porridge steaming in her hands and her lips set in a thin line as she focuses on not spilling any. Her breath comes out in short puffs of steam.

She places the plate by the barn door. From her pocket, she pulls out a wooden spoon and puts it in the plate. "There," she says. "Now you won't be hungry. Merry Christmas, nisser." And she runs back to the house.

In the window, the father follows his daughter with his eyes, a fond smile on his lips.

"She gave us porridge," Nissemor says, her voice shaking with emotion. "Porridge!"

Tulla's gaze goes from me to her mother, clearly confused but also understanding that she's missing something significant.

I take both their hands and pull them over to the steaming plate. "Come," I tell them. "Let's eat while it's still warm. Oh, look at that butter. I don't think I've ever had that much of it before, even in my youth. Would you like to taste it, Tulla?"

For the first time in twenty years, we have our Christmas feast. Our bellies are full of porridge, sugar, and butter, and our hearts full of love and belief.

We're so engrossed in our meal, we miss most of the unpacking of the gifts. When Tulla remembers it, she lurches toward the window, high on butter. She makes a tiny greasy handprint on the glass as she squints toward the Christmas tree.

"It's a sled! I knew it! She's going to have so much fun with that." She burps and seems on the point of falling asleep on her feet.

Nissemor walks up to her. "Maybe it's time for you to go to —"

"She's coming out to test it! She's going to ride the sled straight away! Yesss!"

Tulla takes off toward the front door, sleepiness long forgotten.

"What if one of them sees her?" Nissemor frowns in worry.

"They won't," I tell her. "And if they do, the parents will blame the alcohol and the kids won't really know it's not normal." In any case, they can only see us if they believe in us, so I've been walking around in broad daylight for years. Not that I've ever told Nissemor about it. No need to cause her unnecessary worry.

Two minutes later, the girl comes out the front door, wrapped up in thick winter coveralls, a red bonnet, a blue scarf, and red mittens. She's pulling the brand new red plastic sled behind her and beelines directly for the road. The farm is at the end of the road so there's no risk of any cars coming and the first fifty meters or so are downhill with the perfect incline for a six-year-old to ride her sled.

Tulla runs after her, not wanting to miss a single moment of the fun.

Inside the barn, I hear one of the cows low, in a tone I don't like very much.

"Why don't you go keep an eye on Tulla," I tell Nissemor. "I'm going to check on the cows."

It's Dagros, one of the oldest cows in the barn. She's expecting and the calf is due any day now. In fact, I'm tempted to say it's already on its way.

But something's wrong. The cows, and especially one as experienced as Dagros, know how to give birth on their own. The sounds she's making right now make me think she *doesn't* know what's going on—and that's a bad sign.

I try to help her as well as I can and do my best to calm her but her complaining only gets louder.

I need to get help. I give Dagros a last reassurance before going to the barn door. The thing is very big and heavy for a small nisse like myself but with some effort, I do manage to get it open.

I don't need it open for *me*, of course. I have my secret passages all over the farm. But I know what the humans consider worrisome and worthy of investigation. The barn door standing wide open on a winter night definitely qualifies.

Next, I open the front door. I jump up to grab and lower the handle, then give the door a big push so it slams open.

Then I run and hide in the bushes.

It doesn't take the father more than ten seconds to come to the door. He pokes his head out and yells, "Marie, you know you have to take care with the door..." When his daughter is nowhere in sight and he hears her joyful screams from down the road, he frowns and pokes his head farther outside to try to figure out what caused his door to bang open.

He sees the open barn door. Swears. Closes the door, but comes back out less than a minute later, with a coat and boots on.

I run ahead of him inside the barn and into Dagros's stall. "Come now, Dagros. Moo loudly for the human, will you? He'll be able to help you."

It works. Dagros is louder than ever, and the human comes to check on her instead of just shutting the barn door.

I make a very quick appearance, just to check my theory. There's no reaction from the man, even though I was in his line of sight, so he really can't see me. For this situation, that's a good thing. It means I don't have to keep out of sight.

While the man first goes inside to change, then comes back out and helps the calf get into the right position, I work on calming the cow. She's stressed out about the birth not going like the previous ones, worried about her unborn calf, and in a lot of pain.

Contrary to the people, she *can* see me, and my presence helps. She doesn't kick out at the man who's helping her or step on his feet, which I consider a success.

At one point, I see Nissemor in the barn door, looking rather distressed, but when she sees how busy I am, she turns around and doesn't interrupt us.

An hour later, a beautiful female calf is born. The calf is exhausted, Dagros is exhausted, the man is barely able to stand on his own. But everyone is alive and healthy.

"You go on back to your family," I say softly. "Dagros and I can take it from here."

The man doesn't hear me, not exactly, but he listens anyway. Five minutes later, he's back inside the house, probably getting a shower, while I help Dagros take care of her newborn.

Nissemor comes back to the barn. There's a sheen of sweat on her face and her voice is shaking. "Nissefar," she says. "Please come."

I can't remember if I've ever heard her so afraid before. "What's wrong?" I run out of Dagros's stall and take her in my arms. "Is Tulla okay?"

She shakes her head and breaks out of my embrace, pulls me after her by my hand. "Come see."

As we reach the road, I catch sight of the girl driving down the slope on her sled. She lets out a whoop of joy that must be heard all the way down in the village. I look around, searching for Tulla, who logically shouldn't be very far when one of the kids is having this much fun.

"Where is she?" I ask. "Did something happen to her?" Helping Dagros was important but if Tulla was in danger, getting her out of trouble was *more* important.

Nissemor points down the road, at the sled that has just come to a stop.

The girl gets out of the sled. Holds out a hand—to help Tulla get out.

"She can see her?"

"She not only sees her," Nissemor cries. "She talks to her, touches her, *plays* with her! What are we going to do?"

I'm speechless. I just stand there, watching, as the two children make their way up the hill, the sled trailing behind them. They're *chatting*, the girl gesticulating and Tulla skipping along as if having the time of her life.

"Humans aren't allowed to see nisser," Nissemor says. "What do we do?"

I have no idea.

Then again, who's going to come punish us because a human has seen a nisse? It's not like there's a police for it.

The two girls approach and I step into the shadows of a nearby tree. Nissemor doesn't move.

"She can only see Tulla," Nissemor says.

"Oh." I ease back to stand next to my wife.

The girls get back on the sled, the human girl sheltering our Tulla between her legs, and back down the slope they go, whooping all the way.

"What are they talking about?" I ask.

"They spent about half an hour on the porridge," Nissemor says. "Then another half hour on the other gifts the girl got, with Tulla making suggestions for their use that the parents are *not* going to like. And now they're trying to always drive down the same tracks, to make them as icy as possible, in order to increase their speed."

"Okay." I don't know what else to say.

Some time later, as Orion sits just above the barn and the white owl from down the valley has flown past with two different mice in its beak, the front door opens and the mother comes out to get her daughter back inside.

"But I don't want to, Mamma! I'm having too much fun with the nisse."

The mother chuckles as she stands at the top of the slope, her arms around herself, hands in her armpits, trying to stay warm. "That's great, darling, but it's getting really late and it's time to go to bed. Pappa is already asleep. Did you know Dagros had her calf?"

"She did?" This makes the girl pause. She looks to Tulla. "Did you know about this?"

Tulla shakes her head. "I was here with you, remember?"

"Who are you talking to?" the mother asks.

"The nisse, of course! Told you I was playing with her."

"Okay." With a fond smile, the mother takes the sled and pulls it up to the house. The daughter follows.

"Tulla," I call to my daughter. "You can't risk being seen by anyone else, darling. The game must end here."

She isn't happy about it but she understands. She must know that what happened here tonight was exceptional.

Tulla pulls on the human girl's leg to get her to stop. The girl bends down and the two have a short discussion. The girl looks our way several times, likely because Tulla says we're here, but she can't actually see us. Finally, she nods in acceptance and bends down to give my daughter a hug.

Then she follows her mother inside.

It's just us three nisser, out in the cold winter night, with a sky full of stars and the moon reflecting in the snow, and the weak lowing of the new calf in the barn. We're pretty much in the same situation as we were earlier, staring longingly in at the humans and their holiday feast.

Except we've also had ours. We've eaten enough porridge and butter to last us till next Christmas. We'll keep helping with the animals, getting rid of the rodents. Do our parts around the farm.

And in return, we'll hope that next Christmas, we'll once again get that little taste of magic.

Author's Note

Thank you for reading *The Magic of Sharing*. I wrote this story for an anthology called *Fantastic Christmas*, which was part of WMG Publishing's 2020 Holiday Spectacular, edited by Kristine Kathryn Rusch. If you haven't heard of it, it's an advent calendar type of anthology, where the people signed up get a story in their inbox every day between Thanksgiving and New Year's. This story had the immense honor of being the story selected for Christmas Day. To be fair, that *is* the day the story takes place.

If you enjoy holiday short stories, I strongly recommend picking up the entire volume of *Fantastic Christmas*, or any of its sister volumes. Eleven stories collected per volume, which is available in ebook and print. You can find all the information on the "Anthologies" section of my website.

I also had a story in the 2021 version of *Holiday Spectacular*: *The Case of the Disappearing Gingerbread City*. It's available in the calendar until December 31st 2021, then in ebook during summer 2022, and print in October 2022. It's not as sweet at the story you just read, but more of a fun soft-boiled detective story. With cookies!

To never miss a new release, sign up for my newsletter — it even includes a free story!

R.W. Wallace
rwwallace.com

Also By R.W. Wallace

<u>Mystery</u>

Ghost Detective Novels

Beyond the Grave

Unveiling the Past

Beneath the Surface

Ghost Detective Shorts

Just Desserts

Lost Friends

Family Bonds

Common Ground

Till Death

Family History

Heritage

Eternal Bond

New Beginnings

Severed Ties

Ghost Detective Collections

Unfinished Business, Volume 1

The Tolosa Mystery Series

The Red Brick Haze

The Red Brick Cellars

The Red Brick Basilica

Mystery Collections

Deep Dark Secrets

A Thief in the Night

Time Travel (short stories)

Moneyline Secrets

Family Secrets

Romance

French Office Romance Series

Flirting in Plain Sight

Hiding in Plain Sight

Loving in Plain Sight

Short Stories

Down the Memory Aisle

Holiday Short Stories

Morbier Impossible

A Second Chance

The Magic of Sharing

The Case of the Disappearing Gingerbread City

The Lucia Crown

Down the Memory Aisle

Young Adult Collections

Tales From the Trenches

Science Fiction (short stories)

The Vanguard

Lollapalooza Shorts

Quarantine

Common Enemies

Coiled Danger

Mars Meeting

Adventure (short stories)

Size Matters

About the Author

R.W. Wallace writes in most genres, though she tends to end up in mystery more often than not. Dead bodies keep popping up all over the place whenever she sits down in front of her keyboard.

The stories mostly take place in Norway or France; the country she was born in and the one that has been her home for two decades. Don't ask her why she writes in English—she won't have a sensible answer for you.

Her Ghost Detective short story series appears in *Pulphouse Magazine*, starting in issue #9.

You can find all her books, long and short, all genres, on rwwallace.com.

www.ingramcontent.com/pod-product-compliance
Lightning Source LLC
LaVergne TN
LVHW042045070526
838201LV00077B/805